Cession

By Nisha Pearson

Published by Nielsen Books, 2025.

CESSION

Written by Nisha Pearson.

First edition. February 18, 2025.

Copyright © 2025 Nisha Pearson.

All rights reserved.

This is a work of fiction. Similarities to real people, places, or events are entirely coincidental.

ISBN: 978-1068408106

Contents

This book is dedicated with love and gratitude to my mum, whose constant support has been my anchor; and to my dear Uncle Jake, who has always encouraged me to reach for the stars.

"To see a World in a Grain of Sand,

And a Heaven in a Wild Flower,

Hold Infinity in the palm of your hand,

And Eternity in an hour."

— William Blake,

"Auguries of Innocence"

Chapter 1: The Quiet Before

Lily gazed out the window of her bedroom, the morning sun casting soft light over the suburban streets of Alderwick. It was the kind of town where nothing much happened—just the steady hum of life, punctuated by the occasional car passing by or a distant laugh from a neighbor's garden. But lately, the town had begun to feel different, as though it were holding its breath. Her phone buzzed, snapping her out of her thoughts. A message from Sam:

"Meet me at the woods. Got something to show you."

It was from Sam, her best friend since childhood. He was always up to something, whether it was climbing the old water tower or sneaking into the abandoned library at the edge of town. Today, though, there was a sharp edge to the message, something that made her pause.

Sam had been acting weird the last time she saw him. Pacing, always glancing over his shoulder. "There's something wrong with this town, Lil," he'd whispered, kicking a stone across the pavement. "Like we're all waiting for something to wake up."

Lily grabbed her jacket and glanced at the bookshelf, where her father's latest manuscript lay open, covered in scribbled notes. Beside it sat an old photograph of their family, the edges curling with time. Her mother's eyes, warm and familiar, seemed to follow her. Her dad never talked about her anymore. And the house was never the same since she disappeared. Her dad did his best, but their conversations had become shorter, quieter. He spent most of his time hunched over his laptop, buried in whatever book he was writing.

Maybe it was easier that way.

The streets were quiet as she stepped outside, a faint breeze moving through the trees. Alderwick seemed frozen, waiting for something, and Lily couldn't shake the feeling that whatever it was had already begun.

The woods were only a short walk from her house, but they always seemed further away in the early morning, the path winding through shadows that whispered secrets. The air felt heavy, and the usual chirping of birds was absent, replaced by an unsettling silence.

"Sam?" Her voice broke the stillness, but there was no answer. She stepped further into the woods, each footfall muffled by the damp earth. The further she went, the more the world seemed to blur around her, the sun barely breaking through the canopy above. And then, as she reached the clearing, she saw something that made her pause.

A girl stood at the edge of the woods, her back to Lily. She was tall and slender, with hair that moved like ink in the wind. But it was her eyes—green, deep, and almost unnatural—that held Lily's attention.

When the girl turned, Lily's breath caught in her throat. She looked familiar, but Lily couldn't place where she had seen her before.

"Are you looking for Sam?" the girl asked, her voice soft but unsettlingly calm. Lily's heart slammed against her ribs.

"Who are you? What do you know about Sam?"

The girl's lips curled into a smile that didn't reach her eyes. "He's not here, but he left something for you."

A shiver ran down Lily's spine as the girl held out a small, carved wooden figure—a crescent moon, like the one Sam had made for her. It was warm, as though it had been held just moments ago.

"I'll explain everything. But not here," the girl said, glancing over her shoulder at the forest as if expecting something to emerge from the shadows.

Lily took a hesitant step forward. "Where is he? What's happening?"

The girl's eyes locked with hers, and for a moment, Lily swore she saw a flicker of fear. Then it was gone, replaced by something unreadable.

"I think it's time you found out the truth," the girl whispered.

Chapter 2: The New Girl

The next day, the halls of Alderwick High were thick with the weight of Sam's absence. Students whispered in clusters, casting curious glances at Lily as she made her way to her first class.

She felt their eyes on her but kept her head down, her mind replaying the events of the woods and the girl who had appeared out of nowhere.

Lily slipped into her seat in history class, trying to forget the tightness in her chest. But when the classroom door opened, a hush fell over the room.

A girl stepped in, "The same girl that was in the woods yesterday!" tall and poised, her presence demanding attention. Her hair was so white it almost shimmered, stark against her pale skin. It caught the light in a way that seemed almost unnatural, like a halo or a trick of the sun.

The teacher introduced her as Elara. The new girl's eyes swept the room, landing for a moment on Lily.

There was something familiar about her gaze, sharp and knowing, as if she were seeing through Lily rather than just looking at her. Then, just as quickly, it was gone, replaced by a calm, unreadable expression.

As the class continued, Lily couldn't help but steal glances at Elara. The girl was meticulous, her movements graceful and deliberate.

She didn't engage with anyone, but there was an air of quiet confidence that made Lily's curiosity itch. Elara seemed to be listening to the lesson, but her eyes were often drawn to the window, as if she were waiting for something or scanning the outside world.

It was strange, like she didn't quite belong in the room. And then there was the way she sat—back straight, hands folded on the desk, and a faint, almost imperceptible shimmer to her skin whenever the light hit her just right.

By the end of the day, Lily felt like she knew two things for certain: Elara was not like the other students, and the girl was connected to Sam's disappearance in some way. She couldn't explain why, but every time Elara's eyes met hers, a cold thread of recognition ran through her.

Lily knew she needed answers, but she'd have to be careful. If Elara was part of whatever secret was unravelling in Alderwick, then she needed to find out the truth without drawing attention to herself.

Chapter 3: Unseen Patterns

Lily spent the rest of the school day feeling uneasy. The sight of Elara in every class gnawed at her curiosity, as if the girl were an enigma refusing to be solved. Even when the final bell rang, signaling the end of the day, the unease lingered like a whisper in the back of her mind. She caught sight of Elara in the hallway as she gathered her things.

The girl's hair shimmered as she turned her head, catching the sunlight in a way that made Lily blink. It was too bright, almost unnatural. And then there were the whispers again—students exchanging looks and murmurs.

Elara wasn't just new; she was extraordinary in a way that felt unsettling. As Lily walked out the front doors, she noticed Elara standing by the edge of the schoolyard, gazing at the line of trees that bordered the field. Her expression was distant, eyes unfocused, as though she were looking at something far beyond the horizon.

A chill passed through Lily, prickling the back of her neck. It was the same look she'd seen in the woods when Elara had appeared to her—like she was waiting for something, or someone. "Hey, Lily," a familiar voice said. It was Mia, her friend from English.

She had been calling Lily's name, but the sound had only reached her ears now.

"Are you alright? You've been spaced out all day." "Yeah," Lily said, forcing a smile. "Just... tired."

Mia raised an eyebrow, but before she could say more, Elara's voice reached them from a distance. The words were muffled, but it was clear she was speaking to someone.

Lily's eyes followed the direction of her gaze and landed on a boy standing near the front steps. He was older, maybe a senior, and seemed to be holding something in his hand. For just a moment, Elara's eyes locked with his, a brief moment of recognition passing

9

between them before he turned away, retreating to a group of friends.

That fleeting glance was enough. Lily's pulse quickened. Why did Elara look so familiar, and why did that boy seem to be part of something secretive? Her eyes narrowed as she watched Elara slip inside the building, moving with an otherworldly grace that was both beautiful and eerie.

When Lily arrived home, she couldn't shake the feeling that something was drawing her into the same mystery Sam had been tangled in before he disappeared. She knew she had to find out more about Elara, but not in a way that might make the girl suspicious. Sitting by her desk, Lily rifled through her collection of notes and drawings from past school projects, anything that might give her insight into the stories and secrets Alderwick was known for. But there was something different now, a pattern she couldn't quite place.

The woods, Elara's eyes, the unnatural glow of her hair—everything seemed linked, like pieces of a puzzle she had yet to assemble. A sudden tapping at her window broke her train of thought. She looked up, heart leaping when she saw a figure standing on the lawn outside, shadowed by the trees. It was Elara, watching her from the edge of the woods. This time, Lily didn't look away.

Chapter 4: The Disappearance

The days after Elara's arrival grew heavy with tension. The whispers in the halls of Alderwick High became louder, more urgent. It started with small rumours—how students claimed to hear voices in the woods, or how the night air felt colder than it should. But then the first real disappearance hit, like a strike of lightning.

It was Jess Parker, a girl who sat at the back of Lily's math class. Jess was quiet, always scribbling in her sketchbook and keeping to herself. Nobody had seen her since Monday. The teachers tried to downplay it, attributing her absence to illness or family issues. But by the end of the week, the speculation was too loud to ignore.

"First Sam, now Jess?" Mia whispered to Lily as they sat at their lunch table, the chatter around them too chaotic to make sense of.

"Do you think they're connected?"

Lily's fingers drummed nervously against her tray. "I don't know, but I'm starting to think there's more to Elara than we know."

Mia frowned. "But why her? Why now?"

Before Lily could respond, the lunchroom doors swung open, and Elara walked in, her presence as sharp and unnatural as ever. The murmurs died as she crossed the room, her eyes flickering with that same distant look.

She moved with a grace that felt almost unreal, and it was impossible not to notice the glances she cast toward the windows as though she were searching for something outside. Lily caught the look and felt her heart tighten. The last time she had seen that expression was in the woods, when Elara had been waiting for something. It wasn't just that Elara was different; it was that she didn't belong.

Suddenly, another voice sliced through the tension.

"Hey, did you hear? Marcus Thorne's gone missing too," a student whispered to his friend, barely audible but enough to send a shiver down Lily's spine.

Marcus was popular, known for his easy laugh and quick wit.

The idea that he, too, was gone, felt impossible.

"Not just Sam and Jess," Mia said, her eyes wide. "It's happening again."

Lily stood up, the sound of her chair scraping against the linoleum catching Elara's attention. For a moment, their eyes met, and there was a flicker of recognition in Elara's gaze—something that seemed almost like regret.

Then the moment was gone, replaced by the impassive expression that Lily had grown used to. Lily left the lunchroom, her mind racing. She had to find out what Elara knew, and she had to do it before more kids disappeared. There was no telling how far this would go or what secrets were hiding in the corners of Alderwick. But she knew one thing: Elara was at the center of it, and Lily was determined to figure out why.

Chapter 5: Clues in the Shadows

The sun sank low on the horizon, casting long, angular shadows across the streets of Alderwick. Lily paced her room, glancing nervously out her window. The whispers over the past few days—the rumours about Sam, Jess, and now Marcus—had grown louder, like the echoes of a warning.

It was clear now that something was hiding in the town, something that only she seemed willing to face. Lily pulled open her drawer and sifted through her collection of notes, trying to piece together any connection she might have missed. Scrawled notes about the woods. Sketches of the old, twisted trees.

The unsettling image of Elara's eyes, sharp and too knowing. Her eyes stopped on the last drawing, the figure carved from wood Sam had given her. It had a face too human and yet impossibly alien, with those same deep green eyes. It was almost as if it were watching her. A knock at the door jolted her out of her thoughts. She turned to see her dad in the doorway, his expression soft with concern.

"You've been locked in there for hours, Lily. Is everything okay?"

She nodded, forcing a smile. "Just trying to make sense of things, Dad. It's... it's hard."

He hesitated, then walked over and sat on the edge of her bed.

"I know. Sam was a good kid. But remember, sometimes its better not to dig too deep."

The warning made her heart tighten, but Lily didn't say anything. She couldn't stop now, not when there were so many unanswered questions. As soon as her dad left the room, Lily grabbed her jacket and slipped out the back door.

The air was cool, the evening wind whispering through the trees, almost like it was calling her name. She made her way to the woods that bordered the edge of town. The place where Sam had last been seen. With every step, the crunch of leaves beneath her boots was swallowed by the heavy silence.

She glanced up, half expecting to see Elara standing there, her pale hair glowing in the moonlight. But it was empty. That was until she heard a sound—like a rustle in the underbrush behind her. Heart hammering, she turned sharply.

There, barely visible in the shadows, stood a figure. It was Elara.

"Looking for answers, I see," she said, stepping forward. Her voice was softer than Lily expected, tinged with something unreadable.

"Why did you come here?" Lily demanded, her voice shaking. "And why are kids going missing?"

Elara's eyes, those impossible green eyes that were hard to read, held Lily's gaze.

"Because there's a force in Alderwick that thrives on silence. You've seen it, haven't you? The way the woods call to you, the way the air feels cold and alive."

Lily took a step back. "Why now? Why me?"

Elara's mouth tightened. "Because you're the only one who's not blind to it. And because you might be the only one who can stop it."

Before Lily could ask what she meant, Elara's expression shifted. The faint glow that had been in her eyes dimmed, replaced by a shadow of fear.

"But you need to be careful. If the wrong people know you're looking, they'll come for you."

Lily's breath caught. "What do you mean by 'they'?"

A sudden shout pierced the silence, coming from deeper in the woods. Lily's blood ran cold as she realized it was a voice she recognized—Marcus's.

The sound was cut short, leaving an eerie stillness in its wake.

Elara's eyes were wide, her hand reaching for Lily's arm.

"We need to go. Now." Lily hesitated, torn between following Elara into the woods and finding the source of the scream. But before she could decide, Elara's grip tightened, and she pulled her toward the cover of the trees. As they ran, Lily felt the wind shift, carrying with it a strange, sweet scent. It was the same one she'd smelled the day she first saw Elara. And as they darted deeper into the woods, a distant, unearthly cry echoed behind them. The night seemed to come alive, whispering secrets Lily was afraid to understand.

Chapter 6: Echoes of the Past

The woods behind Alderwick had never felt so alive, and yet so sinister. Lily's heart pounded as Elara led her deeper, avoiding the twisted roots that clawed at the ground like fingers. The sound of the distant cry still reverberated in her ears, cold and hollow.

"What are we looking for?" Lily gasped, glancing sideways at Elara, who seemed to be searching the darkened trees with a practiced eye.

"Clues," Elara said, her voice low. "Things they don't want you to find. But we don't have much time."

Before Lily could ask what she meant, the rustling behind them grew louder. Elara turned slowly, her eyes narrowing as she watched a shadow dart between the trees. Lily's pulse quickened—she'd never been so afraid. The dark seemed to thrum with life, as if something unseen were watching, listening, waiting.

"Who's there?" Elara called into the shadows, the question a challenge.

A low, guttural growl rolled through the trees, so close that Lily could feel it reverberate in her chest. Then, silence. The noise of the forest around them felt too loud, every snap of a twig or hoot of an owl, an invasion of their fragile quiet. Elara grabbed Lily's hand.

"We need to go back. Now." The return journey was rushed and silent, with Elara occasionally glancing back, her expression tense and worried. When they finally stepped back out into the moonlight that spilled over the edge of the woods, Lily's breathing was ragged.

But Elara looked at her with a solemn expression that spoke of warnings yet to come.

"You need to know the truth about Alderwick," Elara whispered, before disappearing into the night as quickly as she had appeared.

Lily stood alone, shaking, the weight of her discoveries pressing down on her like the cold, suffocating fog that rolled in from the woods. What had she just learned? And what did it mean for the town?

Chapter 7: Hidden Memories

That night, Lily lay in bed, unable to sleep. The sound of the wind outside was like a heartbeat, steady and insistent. Her mind returned to a time before Sam and Jess had disappeared, before the eerie quiet had settled over Alderwick. It was when she was little, a memory she had almost forgotten: her mother's voice calling out to her from the kitchen, the warmth of her hand on Lily's forehead as she tucked her in. But then, it was as if her mother had vanished, like a shadow at dusk.

Her father had never spoken about it, but Lily had noticed how the light in his eyes dimmed after that day. A sudden knock at her door startled her. It was her father, his face etched with exhaustion and concern.

He came in and sat down on the edge of her bed, the silence between them heavy.

"I know you're worried about what's happening," he said, his voice low.

"I'm worried too, Lily. You're not the only one looking for answers."

Lily sat up, her heart pounding.

"You know something, don't you, Dad? It's like you've been holding back."

He took a deep breath and looked away, as if the weight of the truth was too much.

"It's not just Sam and Jess. It's... your mother, Lily. I think she was taken, just like them." Lily's eyes widened, the memory of her mother's disappearance rushing back, vivid and painful.

"What do you mean? Why didn't you ever tell me?"

"Because I didn't want you to grow up afraid. But what's happening now... it's the same as before. The woods, the disappearances, the rumours. It's all connected."

Before Lily could respond, a noise outside drew her attention. The faint sound of something skittering in the underbrush, the same sweet scent she'd smelled when Elara had pulled her into the woods. It was too close to ignore.

"Dad, I have to go," she said, urgency creeping into her voice.

He stood, his face darkening with concern.

"Be careful, Lily." But Lily was already moving, racing to find the answers she needed, the secrets that connected her mother's disappearance with the dark, looming force in the woods.

Chapter 8: Secrets and Shadows

Lily darted out of her room, her mind a whirlwind of thoughts. Her father's warning echoed in her ears, but so did Elara's voice: urgent and filled with an unspoken promise. The night air was cool, with a strange heaviness that made her shiver. She slipped into the darkness, determined to find answers. The woods were quieter now, the eerie silence broken only by the sound of her footsteps and the occasional hoot of an owl.

As she moved deeper into the underbrush, her phone buzzed in her pocket. She fished it out, seeing a message from Sam's sister, Mia:

"Please, come back to the woods. I need to know if you found anything."

Lily hesitated, but the thought of Mia's face, pale and hollowed by grief, spurred her onward. It was only then, as she pressed on through the trees, that she noticed the way the air had shifted—a subtle change that made her feel watched. The wind picked up, tugging at her hair as though it knew where she was headed. A figure emerged from the shadows, and Lily's breath caught. It was Elara, standing with her head slightly bowed, as if waiting. The moonlight cut through the darkness, revealing her white-blonde hair, which shone like a beacon.

"You shouldn't be here," Elara whispered, a trace of desperation in her voice. "They will know you're looking."

Lily steadied her breathing, trying to appear braver than she felt.

"I'm not afraid. I just want to understand why Sam and Jess are gone, and why Marcus—" Elara reached out, stopping Lily mid-sentence.

"There's more at stake than you know. And your father—" She hesitated, her eyes shadowed with regret.

"He doesn't know who I am, does he? Not yet. But he will."

Lily frowned, confusion washing over her. "What do you mean?"

Before Elara could answer, a distant noise came from deeper in the woods. It was a low, haunting sound that raised the hair on Lily's arms. Elara stiffened, her eyes narrowing with tension.

"We need to leave," Elara said, but her voice was barely above a whisper.

"Why? What's out there?" Lily demanded, trying to catch a glimpse of whatever had made the noise. Elara turned to look at her, her eyes filled with something Lily couldn't place—fear, maybe, or something darker.

"Something that might be coming for you. Something that's already watching your father." Lily's heart slammed against her ribs. "My dad? What does he have to do with this?"

Elara didn't answer. Instead, she grabbed Lily's hand and pulled her away from the woods, back toward the edge of town. As they moved, Lily felt a prickling sensation at the base of her neck. She glanced back once, but the darkness was empty. Yet the feeling of being followed was unmistakable. By the time they reached the edge of the woods, Lily's legs were weak. She pulled free from Elara's grasp, catching her breath.

"Why did you help me? Who are you really?"

Elara's expression softened, but just for a moment, before it hardened again.

"I'm someone who used to be like you, someone who wants to end this cycle before it's too late."

The forest behind them seemed to hold its breath as if waiting for Elara's next words. But before Lily could press her for more, Elara turned, her pale hair glinting in the moonlight as she slipped into the darkness.

"Lily," her father's voice called from the path behind her. She spun around, eyes wide, and found him there, his face etched with exhaustion and worry.

"Dad," she said, the sound shaky. "We need to talk."

Chapter 9: The Unspoken Truth

Lily's heart raced as she stood face-to-face with her father, who looked as if he'd just aged a year in a single night. The shadows under his eyes were dark, and his hands fidgeted as though they wanted to reach out and hold on to something solid. "Lily," he said again, his voice catching. "Are you alright? I heard voices... and then you weren't in your room."

Lily's eyes darted back toward the woods, her pulse quickening as the image of Elara slipping into the trees burned into her mind. She swallowed hard, forcing herself to stay calm. "I'm fine, Dad. I was just... thinking. About everything."

His gaze narrowed, but instead of questioning her further, he nodded and stepped forward. "We need to talk. About your mother." The sudden change in the conversation sent a chill down Lily's spine.

"What about her?" He sighed, running a hand through his hair, eyes distant and haunted. "Lily. I've been finding things—notes, old photos I kept hidden—but I've never had proof. Now I do, and I'm afraid it's all connected."

Lily felt as though the ground had shifted beneath her, leaving her unsteady.

"Taken? By what? And what does this have to do with Elara?"

He hesitated, looking away as if weighing whether to share the burden with her. "When I first started researching her disappearance, I heard rumours. Whispers of creatures from the woods—things that looked like people, but with eyes that glowed green. I thought they were just stories, but now... now I'm not so sure."

Lily's breath caught. Elara had green eyes. Her hair was as pale as moonlight. Was it possible that Elara was more than she seemed? Before she could ask, her father's expression shifted. He stepped closer, placing a hand on her shoulder.

"Lily, listen to me. If you're involved in this—if you know something—promise me you'll tell me. I can't lose you, not like I lost her."

The weight of his words pressed down on her, almost too much to bear. She wanted to tell him everything, to tell him that Elara had saved her tonight that she had answers, but she couldn't risk it. Not yet. Elara's warnings replayed in her mind. Her father couldn't know Elara's name; it would put them both in danger.

"I promise, Dad," Lily whispered, though the lie sat heavy on her tongue. "I'll tell you everything when the time is right."

He didn't look convinced, but he gave a curt nod.

"Be careful, Lily. This goes deeper than I ever imagined. And I need you to trust me."

Lily squeezed his hand, wishing she could ease his fears. The past was closing in, the threads of her mother's disappearance winding together with the dark secrets of Alderwick, and with Elara, who had appeared at the exact moment Lily's search had begun. But what if the girl with the pale hair and the haunted eyes was not just an ally but a key to unravelling the entire mystery?

A branch cracked behind them, and Lily stiffened. Her father's hand tightened around hers, his eyes darting toward the woods. They were not alone. Lily's voice dropped to a whisper. "Dad, we need to go. Now."

They both turned and started down the path back to the house, the silence following them like a dark promise. The answers were out there, tangled in the forest and in the secrets Elara and Lily's father held close to their hearts. But time was running out, and soon, Lily knew, she would have to decide how much she was willing to risk to find the truth.

Chapter 10: The Hunt for Truth

L ily barely slept that night. The whispers of her father's words haunted her: "I think your mother was taken."

The idea gnawed at her, shifting from denial to a strange, gnawing certainty. When dawn crept through the cracks in her bedroom blinds, she felt the weight of the day pressing down on her. She needed answers. Her father had returned to his study the night before, his exhaustion palpable but his determination sharper than ever. Lily knew he was looking for something that would prove the unthinkable, something that might reveal what had really happened to her mother.

She pushed herself out of bed and tiptoed down the hallway, where she could hear the faint hum of the old kettle in the kitchen. There, her father stood, eyes bloodshot and sleepless, the flicker of a lamp casting a yellow glow over an array of papers spread across the table. Maps of Alderwick, photos from the years before her mother vanished, and crumpled notes filled with half-formed thoughts and angry scribbles.

"What are you looking for, Dad?" Lily whispered, stepping into the room.

His back was to her, and he didn't turn around at first. But when he did, the look on his face was one she'd never seen before: raw, unguarded, and filled with regret and hope.

"It's not what you think, Lily," he said, voice low as if he feared the walls themselves might overhear.

He held up a photo—a grainy picture of her mother with a group of people, all smiling under the bright summer sun. But it was the figure on the far left that caught Lily's eye: a man whose face was blurred, yet whose green eyes seemed to pierce through the paper.

"Dad, who's that?" Lily asked, pointing.

He sighed, looking at her with that same mix of fear and longing.

"That's the man who tried to find your mother. He was an outsider, an investigator who went missing the year after she did. He believed in the bogeymen stories. I didn't think they were real, but after everything that's happened with Sam and the others—"

Lily's pulse quickened. "Bogeymen stories? Dad, are they real?"

He nodded solemnly. "I think they are, Lily. And I think your friend knows more than she lets on."

Chapter 11: The Hidden Truth

Elara didn't come to school the next day. Lily's worry gnawed at her, biting deeper as the hours passed. The absence of the girl with the white-blonde hair made the hallways feel empty and colder than before. It was only when she saw a missed message from Elara that her heart leaped into her throat:

"Meet me at the old library after school. We need to talk."

The library was dark and musty, hidden behind ivy and brick. It had been abandoned for years, a relic of Alderwick's faded glory. Lily's breath came quick as she entered, the quiet creak of the wooden floorboards beneath her feet making her feel exposed.

"Lily," Elara's voice came from the shadows, slow and strained.

The girl stepped into the faint light, her pale hair glowing like a halo. But this time, her eyes weren't cold and calculating.

They were desperate, full of fear. "You're in danger, Lily. If you want to find the truth about your mother, you have to trust me," Elara said, taking a step closer.

Lily met her eyes, searching for any sign of deception. There was none.

"Why should I trust you?" Elara's face fell. "Because I'm not who you think I am. I'm not just here to help you find Sam or the others. I need you to understand that we are all part of a story that's much older than we realize. Your mother was part of it. She knew what I am, what we all are."

Lily's eyes widened, the pieces falling into place. "Then you're—"

"Yes," Elara whispered. "A Boglin. But I'm different. I don't belong to them. I don't want to be like them." Lily stared at Elara, her breath catching in her throat. "A... Boglin?" The word felt unnatural on her tongue. Elara hesitated, then nodded. "We aren't just stories, Lily. We exist. We always have."

Lily shook her head. "But... what are you?"

Elara exhaled, running a hand through her white-blond hair. "Boglins look human, but we're not. We feed on human energy, and we use our mucus to survive. We can hypnotize, manipulate minds. We take children because their energy is... purer. Stronger." Her voice dropped. "That's how we stay young."

Lily's stomach twisted. "You—" She stopped herself. "You've done that?"

Elara's jaw clenched. "I'm half Boglin, Lily. I was born into their world, but I don't want to be like them."

Lily tried to process it. "And the others? The full-blooded ones?"

Elara's green eyes darkened. "They live underground, in swamp caves. They have nests, and once they take someone... it's almost impossible to get them back. They speak without words, through telekinesis.

Elara hesitated, her fingers tightening into fists. "Half-Boglins like me... we have a choice. But if we ever—" She swallowed. "If we ever bond with a full Boglin, we become one of them completely."

Lily frowned. "Bond? What do you mean?"

Elara looked away. "It's how they… continue their kind. If a half-Boglin and a full Boglin connect in that way, the transformation is complete."

Lily's stomach turned. "And you—"

Elara shook her head sharply. "I would never."

For a moment, silence reigned between them, the air so tense Lily could almost hear the thundering of her own heart.

"But why me? Why now?" Lily asked, voice trembling. "Because I saw what was happening to you, to your father. I saw the way they've been hunting the people in this town. Your mother was taken, Lily, because she knew how to stop it. And when she tried, they silenced her."

Elara stepped forward, a tremble in her voice.

"The truth about who I am, who we all are, it's what might save your father and everyone else. But it's also what will make me their enemy."

Lily's world spun. The past and present crashed together, making her dizzy.

"What do you need me to do?" Elara's eyes softened, holding a flicker of hope. "Trust me, and we can stop them. But we need to move fast. There are others who will try to stop us, and the only way to protect everyone is to bring them the truth."

Lily knew this was the moment everything changed. The moment she would either step into the darkness with Elara or run from it, forever questioning what could have been.

Chapter 12: The Shadow Within

Elara took a deep breath as she led Lily deeper into the library, where the air was thick with the scent of mildew and forgotten stories. Books, cracked with age, lined the shelves, their pages yellowed and curling. This was a place for secrets, and Elara was about to share her own.

"You asked why you should trust me, Lily," Elara said, her voice shaking. "The truth is, I'm more like you than I am like them. I'm what they call a 'half-Boglin.'"

Lily's eyes widened, trying to process the words. "Half-Boglin? I don't understand."

Elara walked to the window, fingers brushing the dusty glass as she stared out at the dense woods beyond.

"Boglins are creatures of ancient origin, predating the towns, the stories, even the land itself. They were born from the deep, dark corners of human fear—twisted, unnatural beings that came to be when the balance of nature was disturbed. They look like us, except for their eyes: green, like the depths of a forest after nightfall. And their hair is as white as bone. It's their trademark." Lily shivered, thinking of Elara's striking appearance. The girl who had appeared out of nowhere, the girl who was too beautiful to be real.

"And they... they take children?" Elara nodded, turning to face Lily.

Her eyes, usually sharp and cold, softened with sorrow. "They need to feed on the life force of the young. It keeps them from aging, makes them powerful. They live near the dark, damp places where the earth is thin—swamps, caves, even abandoned forests. They make nests, hideaways where they keep the children they've taken. But if those children try to escape, they hunt them down. No one has ever returned."

Lily's breath caught in her throat. "But why... why would someone like you be here, and why are you helping me?"

Elara took a step closer, the space between them closing, but her eyes grew distant as she spoke.

"Because I was born of both human and Boglin. My mother was taken by them years ago, and my father, a human, was left to grieve and search for answers. He raised me knowing I was different, but he never told me why."

Elara's fingers curled into the fabric of her sleeve. "My mother... she was a Boglin," she admitted, voice barely above a whisper. "My father was human. He didn't know what she really was—not at first. By the time he found out, it was too late."

Lily's breath caught. "Too late for what?"

Elara hesitated. "For him to stop loving her. For him to leave." She exhaled shakily. "Boglins don't feel emotions like humans do, but... my mother stayed with him longer than she should have. Maybe that means something. Maybe it doesn't."

I only learned the truth when I was older—when I began to feel the call of their dark power, the urge to join them. I fought it. I chose to be human, to save what I could of myself. But that choice came with a price. The Boglins want me back, and if they find out I'm aiding you, they'll come for us both."

Lily's mind spun as she took in everything Elara said. Half-Boglin. A creature born of two worlds, forced to live between the shadows and the light. And it explained everything—the secrets, the cold, distant look in her eyes, the pale hair like a shroud.

"What do you mean, 'they'll come for us'?" Lily whispered, the words heavy with fear. Elara's lips tightened. "It's not just a myth, Lily. They are real. The Boglins are more than just stories to scare children; they are predators. They can hypnotize their prey, making them forget, making them trust. And when they find you, they use their tendrils—long, dark appendages that reveal their true forms—to draw you into their world. A world where they can drain your essence and hold you forever."

The room grew colder, and Lily's heartbeat thundered in her ears. The Boglins weren't just a distant threat; they were alive and closing in. "But you're not like them," Lily said, desperation breaking through her voice.

"You have to know how to stop them, Elara. You have to."

Elara's expression darkened. "There is a way. A secret that has been lost for centuries. A way to break their hold, but it's dangerous. If we fail, they will hunt us down and take everything we hold dear."

Lily reached out, grabbing Elara's hand. The warmth of her touch was reassuring, grounding. "Then we do it together. We find the secret and stop them, no matter what it takes."

Elara looked at her with a mix of admiration and sadness, as if she had just heard something she'd wanted to hear for a long time. "Then we start by gathering the stories. The old tales your mother kept hidden. She knew something, Lily, and it's time we found out what it was."

The truth about Elara's identity wasn't just a burden; it was the key to saving Alderwick and everyone who lived there. And as Lily and Elara prepared to take their first step into a world that was more dangerous than either had ever imagined, one thing was certain: the fight against the Boglins was about to begin.

Chapter 13: Gifts of the Unseen

Elara's eyes flickered with a mixture of vulnerability and power as she spoke, revealing truths that were woven into the very fabric of her being. "Being half-Boglin isn't just a curse; it's a gift. I can sense their presence before anyone else can. I can hear the whispers of the celium when they call to each other. And I can touch the barrier between our worlds."

Lily's heart raced at the mention of the celium, the hidden network through which Boglins traveled, an ancient, living thread that connected the dark places of the world.

"What does that mean for us?" she asked, trying to steady her breathing. Elara's gaze was distant, a shadow of pain crossing her features.

"It means I can lead us through the hidden paths. The celium has many routes, but only those born with their essence can traverse it. The Boglins, however, know the pathways better than anyone. They can see through the barrier, like ghosts with eyes that can pierce through the night."

Lily thought of the stories her mother used to tell her, tales of shadows that moved independently, of whispers that led you astray. Now she realized those were more than just stories; they were warnings.

"But there's more," Elara continued, her voice softening. "The Boglins have the power to read minds and twist emotions.

They take away memories, making their victims forget the past. That's why they can be so convincing and dangerous; they don't just hunt with brute force, they prey on trust."

Lily shivered, remembering how the new girl at school, Elara, had seemed to appear when Sam went missing, as if she had emerged from the fog, ready to fill a void. Elara was right—her presence had been comforting but unsettling, as though she knew secrets Lily didn't.

Chapter 14: The Hidden Power

E lara's half-Boglin gifts were subtle but potent. When she was calm, a silvery glow would briefly spark around her hands, like moonlight on water. If she focused, she could reach out through the celium, pulling visions and whispers from the dark. It was this ability that would be their greatest weapon, but also their greatest risk.

"We have to learn how to harness it," Elara said. "There's a place in Alderwick where the veil between our world and theirs is thin. My mother found it long ago and used it to keep their attention away from us. But it's guarded by the old spirits, and they're not kind to trespassers."

The idea of facing whatever guardians protected the veil sent a shiver down Lily's spine.

"What are these guardians?" she asked.

"Half-formed, creatures that have never fully transitioned. They are not fully sentient, but they're twisted, as if caught between two worlds. They serve as the gatekeepers, using their own telepathic wails to disorient intruders."

"But you can handle them, right?" Lily said, her voice wavering between hope and doubt. Elara's eyes met hers, a mix of strength and uncertainty. "I can, but only if I'm not overwhelmed by their influence. If I lose control, I could become one of them." The weight of that admission pressed heavily on Lily. Elara wasn't just guiding them; she was risking everything, her identity, her sanity, to help save Alderwick.

Chapter 15: The Truth about Boglins

Lily sat cross-legged on the floor of her dad's study, surrounded by a maze of open books, newspaper clippings, and his meticulously scrawled notes. The warm glow of the desk lamp spilled over the pages, illuminating centuries of folklore that had quietly whispered warnings about creatures like the Boglins.

Her father sat at his desk, his brow furrowed in thought, flipping through an ancient tome with care.

"I don't get it," Lily said, brushing her hair out of her face. "If Boglins are real, why doesn't anyone know about them? Why don't people warn others?"

Her father leaned back in his chair, tapping a pen against his palm. "They do," he replied. "Just not directly. The stories are there, hidden in folklore, distorted over time, but all connected if you know what to look for. Boglins are what some cultures might call bogeymen."

Lily frowned. "Bogeymen? Like the thing parents use to scare kids into behaving?"

"Yes," he said, nodding. "But they're not just myths meant to scare children. They've been known by different names in different places—always lurking in the dark, stealing the vulnerable, and feeding off fear. Every culture has a version of them. In Germany, there's the Schwarze Mann, or 'Black Man,' who hides in the shadows. In Sweden, there's Bäckahästen, a malevolent creature tied to water that lures children to their doom. Even here in England, stories of the bogeyman are old as dirt, tied to the swampy, misty places of our countryside."

Lily traced a finger over one of the illustrations in front of her—a tall, wiry figure with elongated limbs and glowing eyes. "What about... Slender Man?" she asked hesitantly.

Her dad glanced at the image she was looking at. "Modern invention, sure, but the essence of it comes from something ancient. Tendrils, the ability to hypnotize or control people, the way it preys on the young—there's a reason it resonates so strongly. It's an echo of what's been known for millennia."

"But Boglins aren't just stories, are they?" Lily murmured. Her father shook his head solemnly.

"No. They've always been real. And the evidence is out there if you know where to look. Even the ancient Egyptians might have known about them." Lily's eyes widened. "The Egyptians?"

He leaned forward, pulling out a grainy black-and-white photo of a crumbling tomb wall. "See this?" he said, pointing to a hieroglyph. The image depicted a man with elongated limbs and something protruding from his back—thin, spiraling shapes that could only be described as tendrils.

"These carvings are over 4,000 years old. Archaeologists chalk it up to artistic interpretation or ritual symbolism, but I'm not so sure. There are similar depictions in Mesopotamian carvings, too, and even in

Native American petroglyphs. Whatever these creatures are—Boglins, bogeymen, or something else—they've been haunting humanity since the dawn of time."

Lily stared at the hieroglyph, her stomach twisting. The idea that something so terrifying could stretch back to ancient civilizations made the threat of the Boglins feel even more real.

"What did the Egyptians think they were?"

"Hard to say," her father admitted. "Some think they were seen as guardians of the underworld, something to fear and appease. Others argue they were predators, pure and simple, slipping into the mortal world to snatch the living. The tendrils—" he gestured to the carving, "—might symbolize their otherworldly power, the way they change form when their disguise drops."

Lily leaned back, her mind racing. "If they've been around this long, why hasn't anyone figured out how to stop them?"

"Maybe they did," her dad said quietly, his voice tinged with an edge of hope. "Maybe that's why the stories exist—to warn us, to remind us. Somewhere out there, the key to stopping them might already exist. We just have to find it."

Lily thought of Elara, of her green eyes that seemed so alive yet so alien. Could she really trust her? Or was Elara just another trap in the long game the Boglins had been playing since ancient times?

For now, all Lily could do was keep searching, keep fighting—and hope that the stories held more answers than fears.

Chapter 16: The Fight Within

As Elara trained Lily in the hidden room of the library, the two girls practiced their focus. The room was dim, the only light coming from the small lantern Elara had brought. She taught Lily to sense when the air grew thick and electric, when the silence that came before a Boglin attack fell over them like a shroud.

"You can feel it, right?" Elara said. Lily nodded, feeling a tremble in the air, a subtle pull that made her hair stand on end. It was the call of the celium, a reminder that they were standing on the edge of a world where shadows reigned and whispers could kill. Elara's eyes blazed with determination. "This is our only chance. If we can hold our ground, we can confront them and find out what really happened to your mother."

Lily met Elara's gaze, seeing for the first time the rawness in her eyes—the part of her that was still human, still fighting.

"We can do this," Lily whispered, knowing that even if Elara had been born of the dark, there was a spark in her that refused to be snuffed out.

Chapter 17: The Gathering Storm

The library had become their fortress, filled with ancient books, maps, and scribbled notes. Elara and Lily had worked tirelessly over the past week, piecing together what little they knew.

The town of Alderwick, with its twisting alleys and overgrown woods, was hiding more than just the Boglins. It was concealing a dark truth that stretched back centuries. Elara's knowledge of the Boglins' strengths and weaknesses was invaluable. She taught Lily how to shield her thoughts and stay calm under pressure.

"Fear feeds them," she warned. "They can sense it like a predator sensing prey. If you let them see that you're afraid, they'll strike before you're ready."

Lily nodded, her pulse thudding in her ears. She had never felt more alive, more aware of her own strength. The search for Sam, the encounters with Elara, and the clues she had gathered had all led to this moment. The night they would confront the Boglins.

Chapter 18: The Veil's Edge

The sky was a deep shade of indigo as they made their way to the edge of the forest. Elara led the way, her movements swift and quiet. The air was damp and cool, carrying with it the scent of wet earth and the faint rustle of hidden life. They reached an ancient stone circle, half-hidden by ivy and moss. It was said to be the entrance to the veil, the barrier between the human world and the realm of the Boglins.

Lily's breath quickened as Elara placed her hand on the stone at the center of the circle. The air shimmered around them, as though reality itself was bending. Elara turned to Lily, her eyes serious and filled with a silent promise.

"Once we go in, there's no turning back. We have to stick together."

Lily swallowed hard, nodding. "I know."

Elara whispered an incantation in a language Lily didn't recognize. The air cracked like lightning, and the world rippled before them. It was like stepping into a new dimension, where the colours were too vivid, and the light felt like it was alive.

The Boglin world was beautiful in a way that was terrifying, filled with trees that had black bark and leaves that dripped silver. The ground felt slick underfoot, as though it was coated in a thin layer of liquid. As they moved deeper into the realm, they saw the first signs of the Boglins—glimpses of movement in the shadows and the low, rhythmic hum of their telepathic chatter. Elara's eyes darted around, her senses on edge. Elara's breath hitched as the shadows shifted around her. She could feel them, calling her name through the celium, their voices curling like smoke in her mind. Her fingertips tingled, her vision sharpened—then Lily touched her arm, and the sensation vanished.

"You okay?" Lily asked.

Elara forced a smile. 'Yeah. Just tired.' A lie. "Stay close to me," she whispered, gripping Lily's hand. "They can sense us, but if we're together, they won't know who to target first."

Chapter 19: The Guardians of the Veil

A sharp, high-pitched cry split the air, making Lily freeze. Elara's face turned pale as a figure emerged from the darkness. It was half-formed, eyes wide and filled with a hollow, unnatural light. Its limbs were thin, elongated, and its skin was an unsettling mix of human and something far more sinister.

This was the guardian Elara had warned her about. Before they could react, more figures appeared, their twisted forms shifting and flitting just out of sight, waiting for a chance to strike. Lily's heart raced as she looked to Elara, whose eyes were dark pools of focus and fear.

"Stay with me," Elara said, the calm in her voice belied by the tremor in her fingers. "They haven't fully transitioned. They are weak, but they can still overpower us if we're not careful." The air thickened as the guardians closed in, their movements impossibly fast. Elara raised her hand, and the silvery glow enveloped her like an armour.

She whispered something, a string of words that resonated with the power of the old world. The guardians shrieked, their forms contorting as they struggled against the barrier Elara summoned. "Run, Lily!" Elara shouted. "Get to the hidden bubble. It's our only chance!"

Chapter 20: The Hidden Bubble

Lily sprinted ahead, heart pounding as she followed Elara's instructions. The hidden bubble was said to be protected by the last vestiges of the spirits who had once lived in harmony with the Boglins.

It was their sanctuary, a place that could shield them and, if necessary, send them back to the human world. The guardians were relentless, shrieking and howling behind them, but Elara's power carved a path through the chaos. When they reached the bubble, it shimmered like liquid glass, a gateway of green light that pulsed with the rhythm of a heartbeat.

"They'll be drawn to it," Elara gasped, her strength waning. "If they breach it, they could die."

Lily glanced back and saw the guardians closing in. But at that moment, Elara's eyes met hers, and she saw something new: a flash of hope. Elara's voice cracked as she spoke.

"Go, Lily! Now!" Lily hesitated, torn between saving herself and saving Elara. But as the guardians lunged, Elara's light flared brightly, creating a barrier that engulfed her.

The world spun as Lily dove into the bubble, the last thing she saw was Elara, a determined smile on her lips before the barrier split and swallowed her up. She emerged back in the human world, breathless and shaken, her mind reeling with the memory of Elara's sacrifice. The night was quiet, the forest still and unmoving, but Lily knew the fight was far from over.

Chapter 21: The Return and the Silence

Lily stood in the moonlight, her body trembling and eyes wide with shock. The forest behind her was dark, silent as though holding its breath. She was alone, or so it seemed, with only the memory of Elara's sacrifice echoing in her mind. The green glow of the bubble had faded, leaving no trace of the world she had just left behind.

"Lily," a familiar voice called out from the shadows. It was her father, his face lined with worry as he stepped into view, clutching his notebook like a shield. "I heard something—are you okay?"

Lily could only nod, her lips too dry to speak. The absence of Elara's presence pressed on her chest like a weight. She needed to tell her father everything, but there was a question that still gnawed at her: Was Elara alive?

"Dad," she managed, her voice cracking, "we need to talk.

About the forest, about the disappearances... about Mum."

Her father's eyes flickered with the ghost of old pain. "I know," he said, taking her hand. "I've suspected for a long time that she was taken, but I didn't want to believe it. The stories... the Boglins... I thought they were just that—stories."

"They are real," Lily whispered, her heart heavy. "And Elara—she's... she's still there, but I don't know how long she'll survive."

Her father's grip tightened, a spark of determination igniting behind his eyes. "Then we find a way to bring her back. We'll need help, Lily. The kind of help no one believes we can get."

Chapter 22: A Glimpse in the Dark

Back in the Boglin realm, Elara was chained in a cavernous chamber with walls that seemed to pulse with a life of their own. The guardians, half-Boglins with twisted forms, loomed over her, their telepathic whispers like claws scraping across her mind.

The full Boglins, regal and terrifying with their sharp, green eyes, surrounded her, their long white-blonde hair a halo of dread.

"You have betrayed your kin," a voice spoke from the darkness. The leader of the Boglins stepped forward, her eyes deep wells of green.

"You protected the human girl, and now you will suffer." Elara met her gaze, her heart pounding with both fear and defiance.

"I did what was right. You're not leaders, you're captors. You don't deserve power."

A sudden, sharp cry echoed through the chamber. Elara's eyes widened as she sensed it—Lily calling out to her in the way they did when they were connected, even across dimensions. The memories of the human world, of laughter and sunlight, surged through her like a lifeline.

"You can't escape," the leader said, her voice a low, venomous hiss. But Elara could feel the faint pulse of hope. It was like a heartbeat in the dark, signaling that this wasn't the end. Outside the chamber, hidden in the shadows, the feelers gathered.

Chapter 23: The Fight for Elara

Back in Alderwick, Lily and her father gathered with a group of allies who were just as determined to fight. The feelers had come to their side—silent, watchful figures with eyes that seemed to see through the shadows of the world. They had faced the Boglins before and survived. Now, they would help Lily find Elara and free her from the prison of the Boglin realm.

Lily turned towards Jace, the leader of the feelers. He stood slightly apart from the group, arms crossed, and his dark eyes sharp with quiet intensity. A thin scar ran along his jawline, disappearing beneath the collar of his warn leather jacket. He looked like someone who had seen too much, someone who had survived things others wouldn't believe.

"We need to move fast," Jace said, his voice low but firm. "The Boglins know we're coming."

"We need to get there before it's too late," Lily said, gripping the green talisman Jace had handed her. It pulsed faintly in her palm, its energy both comforting and ominous.

"This will open the path," Jace said. "But be warned—the Boglins will sense us coming. Stay strong. Their tricks can deceive even the sharpest mind."

Jace rolled up his sleeve, revealing a thin, silver scar running from his wrist to his elbow. "They almost took me when I was eight. I remember their voices in my head, whispering things I knew weren't real. My mother broke their hold before they could finish. She didn't make it." He exhaled sharply. "That's why I fight. So no one else ends up like her."

The group stepped into the dense forest at the edge of town, the air thick with the scent of conifer trees. The breeze carried a sweetness that made Lily pause. It was intoxicating, almost serene, but she shook her head, trying to stay focused. "Don't breathe it in too deeply," Jace warned. "It's part of their lure."

The forest seemed to tighten around them as the talisman's glow intensified. The trees loomed taller, their branches twisting unnaturally. The air grew colder, yet the sweet fragrance remained, clinging to Lily like a memory she couldn't place.

As they crossed the threshold into the Boglin world, the landscape shifted into something alien. The ground beneath them pulsed like a living thing, and the conifer scent was stronger now, almost suffocating.

"Lily," a voice called from the shadows ahead.

She froze. It was Sam. He emerged from the murk, his face pale but familiar, his eyes wide with desperation. "Lily, thank God. I've been trapped here for so long," he said, reaching out to her. "I need your help. We need to get out of here before they come back."

Her heart twisted. Sam's voice, his face—it was all so painfully real. She took a step toward him, her grip on the talisman loosening.

"Don't," Jace said sharply, stepping in front of her.

"But its Sam," Lily insisted, her voice cracking.

Jace's expression hardened. "Look closer."

Lily hesitated, her eyes narrowing as she studied Sam. That's when she saw it—his shadow didn't move naturally, and his eyes, though brown at first glance, gleamed faintly green in the dim light.

"You're not him," Lily whispered, her voice trembling.

"Lily, it's me," the figure pleaded, taking another step toward her.

"No," she said, stepping back. Her voice grew stronger. "You're one of them."

The figure's expression twisted into something inhuman, the illusion shattering as tendrils erupted from its back, lashing out toward her. Jace raised a hand, and the feelers sprang into action, surrounding the creature. Their presence was like a storm of raw emotion, forcing the Boglin back. It shrieked as the tendrils recoiled, its form shifting chaotically before it vanished into the shadows.

Lily's breath came in short gasps, the talisman in her hand glowing fiercely once more.

"Stay focused," Jace said. "They'll do anything to break you." As they pressed deeper into the Boglin realm, the oppressive atmosphere intensified. The sweet conifer scent mingled with a strange hum that vibrated through Lily's chest. The ground beneath their feet seemed to breathe, as if the entire realm was alive and watching them.

Suddenly, the group entered a massive chamber illuminated by an eerie green light. The Boglins hissed and recoiled at the sight of the feelers, their twisted forms quivering. Lily realized why: the feelers weren't just immune to the Boglins' hypnotism—they made the Boglins feel.

For creatures that had never known love, guilt, or fear, the sudden rush of emotion was unbearable. It broke their concentration, left them vulnerable, and made them lash out in confusion and rage.

Jace stepped forward, his presence commanding. "Spread out!" he ordered the feelers. They moved swiftly, their calm, deliberate actions sending waves of emotional resonance through the chamber.

The Boglins recoiled further, their tendrils flailing as if trying to escape the intangible force that rattled them to their core.

In the center of the chamber, restrained by glowing tendrils, was Elara. Her white-blonde hair was tangled, her usually sharp eyes dulled by exhaustion.

"Elara!" Lily called out, her voice cutting through the chaos. Elara's head snapped up, a flicker of recognition crossing her face.

"Lily?" Without hesitation, Lily rushed forward, clutching the talisman tightly. The green glow intensified, pushing back the tendrils that held Elara captive.

As she reached her, Elara collapsed into her arms, trembling but alive. "You came," Elara whispered, her voice hoarse but filled with relief.

"Always," Lily replied, her grip tightening. The chamber began to shake violently as the leader of the Boglins appeared, her towering form casting a shadow over them all.

Her voice was a thunderous roar. "You dare defy me in my own domain?"

Jace and the feelers formed a protective circle around Lily and Elara. The talisman in Lily's hand flared brighter, its warmth giving her strength.

"This isn't over," the leader snarled, her power surging like a tidal wave. The chamber began to crumble under the strain, the ground splitting open as the fight reached its peak.

"Hold on!" Jace shouted, as the feelers pushed back against the Boglins' assault.

Lily pulled Elara into an embrace, holding her close. "We're not done yet. We're going home."

But the leader of the Boglins roared, her power surging like an electric current. "This isn't over," she said, as the chamber began to collapse under the weight of the struggle. Jace and the feelers closed ranks, their presence keeping the Boglins at bay.

The green glow of the talisman burned brighter, a beacon of hope in the chaos. Lily held Elara tighter, refusing to let her go as they prepared to make their escape.

Chapter 24: The Moment Before Dawn

The world spun as they fought their way back through the veil, the power of the talisman pulling them through. When they emerged in Alderwick, the forest was dark and still, but the echoes of battle lingered in the air. Elara fell to her knees, gasping, but Lily reached out, steadying her.

"You're safe now." Elara managed a weak smile, her hand touching Lily's cheek.

"For now. But we're only just beginning."

They both looked up at the night sky, where the stars seemed to tremble in response to the chaos that had just occurred. Somewhere, in the dark reaches of the Boglin realm, the leader's eyes glimmered with malice. But for now, there was hope—a small, fierce light that refused to go out.

Chapter 25: The Dawn of Reckoning

Lily sat by the window, staring out at the stars as they blinked in the inky sky. The village of Alderwick seemed unchanged, but everything inside her had shifted. Elara lay on the couch, wrapped in blankets, her white-blonde hair tangled and her eyes sunken but brighter than before. Lily could see the exhaustion etched into every line of her face. They were safe, for now. But the weight of what had just happened pressed down on them both.

"Elara," Lily whispered, her voice cracking with emotion. "What happens now?"

Elara looked up, her green eyes meeting Lily's. There was a storm in those eyes, a mix of fear and determination.

"The Boglins will come for us. They know we're a threat now.

We need to be ready."

Lily swallowed hard, glancing over at her father, who was still awake, poring over his notes in the living room. The stories he'd once scoffed at now seemed less like fiction and more like prophecy.

The Boglins were real, and they had a reason to come after them. But why had Elara risked everything for her? It was a question that gnawed at Lily, and she knew she needed to ask. "Why did you protect me?" Lily finally asked, her voice barely above a whisper. Elara's lips twitched into a half-smile.

"Because you're worth it, Lily. You have the strength to do what no one else can. You're not just a girl. You're the key to ending this."

Lily felt a surge of heat in her chest at Elara's words. "I don't know if I'm ready for this. But I'm not going to stop fighting. I promise."

Elara reached out, gripping Lily's hand.

"Then we'll face it together. The Feelers will help us, but we'll need more than just them. We need to find out who's pulling the strings in the Boglin realm."

Chapter 26: The Unseen Puppet

In the dim, shifting world of the Boglins, the leader known as Mavaron stood before a dark altar carved from the bones of ancient creatures. The flickering green glow of the chamber illuminated her face, revealing twisted features and eyes that glowed with malice. At her feet, a swirling pool of liquid light reflected the struggles of those trapped in his grasp.

"They think they've won," Mavaron said, his voice a cold rasp.

"But they don't know what's coming."

A figure stepped forward from the shadows—Elara's mother, her movements fluid and inhuman. Her pale, nearly translucent skin shimmered faintly in the green light, and her unnaturally white-blonde hair framed her sharp features. Her eyes, an intense green, glowed faintly as she regarded Mavaron with cold detachment.

"Mavaron," she said, her voice devoid of emotion but steady. "The girl... she will not stop. You have underestimated her." Mavaron's lips twisted into a cruel smile. "Let them come. The world they know is about to unravel."

Nearby, a young girl sat cross-legged on the cold stone floor, her head tilted back slightly as if basking in an unseen warmth. She wore a serene, dreamlike expression, her small frame relaxed and vulnerable.

Mavaron turned toward her, tendrils unfurling like dark, glistening ribbons. They moved with an unnatural grace, extending and latching onto the girl's forehead, mouth, and sides. Her body sagged further, her expression blissful as though she were lost in a comforting dream. Elara's mother watched without a flicker of emotion, her posture unmoving, her gaze fixed on Mavaron. To her, this was not horror but necessity—a part of the endless cycle that kept their kind alive.

The tendrils pulsed faintly, drawing out the girl's life force. Her skin grew pale, her small body shrinking as her vitality drained into Mavaron.

She remained hypnotized by the illusion of warmth and love, unaware of her true fate. Finally, as the last threads of her essence were consumed, her lifeless body collapsed inward, leaving only a brittle shell behind.

Mavaron retracted his tendrils and turned back to Elara's mother.

"Do you see?" she said, her voice a low hiss. "This is balance. This is power. And this is how we will endure."

Elara's mother inclined her head slightly, her face as impassive as before. "You may be right," she said. "But balance is a delicate thing, Mavaron. Even the strongest structures can crumble under the right pressure."

Mavaron's glowing eyes narrowed. "Then let them try."

Chapter 27: The Gathering Storm

The days passed in a blur of whispered meetings and urgent plans. Lily and Elara worked with the Feelers, sharing stories and piecing together the history of the Boglins. It was a story marked by treachery, hunger, and a relentless cycle of power. But Lily had a fire inside her now, a reason to keep fighting. Her father had put aside his doubts and joined their efforts, helping to craft traps and barriers using ancient methods that even the Boglins would not expect.

One evening, Elara pulled Lily aside as the wind howled through the forest outside. "We need to go to the heart of their realm,"

Elara said, her voice steady but filled with tension. "There's a secret there, something that could end this."

Lily met Elara's eyes, seeing the weight of her words. "We're going back?" Elara nodded. "But this time, we're going to bring everyone. We need to be strong enough to face Mavron and whatever she's planning."

Chapter 28: Into the Abyss

The Feelers, now a united front, stood at the edge of the forest with Lily, Elara, and her father. The night air felt charged with electricity as they prepared for the journey. Jace, the leader of the Feelers, stepped forward, his eyes scanning the faces around him.

"We don't know what lies beyond. But we do know this: if we go, we go together." With a deep breath, Lily took Elara's hand and stepped forward, feeling the pulse of the talisman in her pocket. It was time to face what had been hidden for so long.

The world spun, the air crackled, and they stepped into the Boglin realm once more.

Chapter 29: The Battle of Shadows

The realm was dark, a labyrinth of damp caves and twisted roots that pulsed like veins. The group pressed forward, their voices a chorus of determination and unity. Suddenly, the ground quaked, and a deep, guttural roar echoed through the tunnels. Mavron appeared, surrounded by the full Boglins, their eyes blazing with unfeeling hunger.

"Welcome back," Mavron sneered.

"Did you really think you could stop me?" Lily's heart pounded in her chest, but she stood taller, Elara's hand in hers.

"We're here to end this, Mavron. No more secrets, no more fear."

The battle that ensued was one of chaos and courage. The Feelers moved with a precision that made the Boglins falter, their powers forcing the creatures to feel emotions they had never known. The white-blonde hair of the Boglins glistened like the moon, and the green eyes of their leaders burned brighter as they clashed with the invading force.

But Elara's voice cut through the noise, a command that stilled even the most powerful Boglins.

"Lily, now! The altar! We need to destroy it!"

Lily charged forward, her heart in her throat as she grabbed the talisman and raised it high. The glow expanded, a burst of light that surged through the chamber, cutting through the darkness.

Mavron screamed, her form dissolving into the void, his power flickering out like a dying ember.

Chapter 30: The Aftermath and the Promise

The battle was over, but the cost was steep. The chamber fell silent, and the Boglins who remained stood in confusion, their green eyes dimming. Lily and Elara, exhausted and bloodied, stood side by side. The talisman pulsed one last time before shattering into a million tiny, glowing shards.

"Did we do it?" Lily asked, her voice barely audible. Elara looked out at the dawn breaking across the horizon, the sky painted in hues of gold and pink.

"We stopped Mavron. But there's more to do. The Boglins are still here, but now they know they can be defeated."

Lily turned to Elara, their breath mingling in the cold night air. The battle was over—for now—but something between them had shifted.

Elara hesitated, her gaze searching Lily's face. "You didn't have to come back for me," she murmured, voice quieter than usual.

Lily swallowed, the weight of everything pressing against her chest. "Of course I did."

A flicker of something passed through Elara's expression—gratitude, relief, something deeper. Her fingers brushed Lily's wrist, lingering just a second too long. A warmth spread through Lily's skin, an unspoken question hanging between them.

For the first time, neither of them looked away.

As the sun rose, Lily felt hope bloom in her chest, a promise that as long as they stood together, they could face whatever came next. Elara's eyes met Lily's, and in that moment, with the forest quiet and the wind carrying whispers of the past, they knew this was not the end. It was the beginning of something greater—a world where darkness and light could coexist, where courage outshone fear. And somewhere, in the distance, a new story was beginning to be written.

About the Author

Nisha Pearson is an actor, writer, and occasional promotional model from Surrey, nestled in the southeast of London. With a degree in Literary Theory from St Mary's University, Nisha has honed her craft in storytelling, blending academic insight with her creative passions.

As an avid film buff, she finds endless joy and inspiration in cinema, often channeling her love for film into her writing and performances.

For updates on her latest projects or a glimpse into her creative world, you can follow her on Instagram: @lilli_expressions

BOOKS SIMILAR TO *CESSION*

An Ember in the Ashes
by Sabaa Tahir

An Ember in the Ashes is the book everyone is talking about.

Under the Martial Empire, defiance is met with death.

When Laia's grandparents are brutally murdered and her brother arrested for treason by the empire, the only people she has left to turn are the rebels.

But in exchange for their help in saving her brother, they demand that Laia spy on the ruthless Commandant of Blackcliff, the Empire's greatest military academy. Should she fail, it's more than her brother's freedom at risk... Laia's very life is at stake.

There, she meets Elias, the academy's finest soldier. But Elias wants only to be free of the tyranny he's being trained to enforce. He and Laia will soon realise that their destinies are intertwined—and that their choices will change the fate of the Empire itself.

Girls of Paper and Fire
by Natasha Ngan

In this richly developed fantasy, Lei is a member of the Paper caste, the lowest and most persecuted class of people in Ikhara. She lives in a remote village with her father, where the decade-old trauma of watching her mother snatched by royal guards for an unknown fate still haunts her.

Now, the guards are back and this time it's Lei they're after — the girl with the golden eyes whose rumoured beauty has piqued the king's interest.